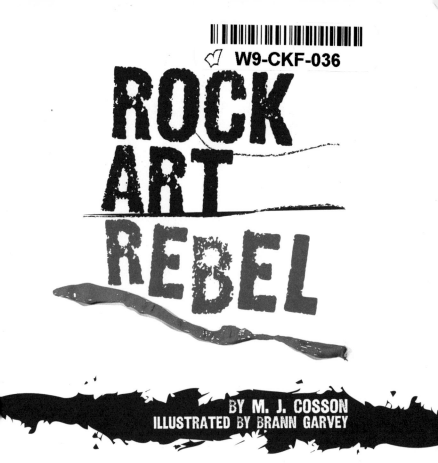

ROCK ART REBEL

BY M. J. COSSON
ILLUSTRATED BY BRANN GARVEY

Librarian Reviewer
Marci Peschke
Librarian, Dallas Independent School District
M.A. Education Reading Specialist, Stephen F. Austin State University
Learning Resources Endorsement, Texas Women's University

Reading Consultant
Mark DeYoung
Classroom Teacher, Edina Public Schools, MN
B.A. in Elementary Education, Central College
M.S. in Curriculum & Instruction, University of MN

STONE ARCH BOOKS
Minneapolis San Diego

Vortex Books are published by Stone Arch Books
151 Good Counsel Drive, P.O. Box 669
Mankato, Minnesota 56002
www.stonearchbooks.com

Library of Congress Cataloging-in-Publication Data
Cosson, M. J.
    Rock Art Rebel / by M. J. Cosson; illustrated by Brann Garvey.
    p. cm. — (Vortex Books)
    Summary: As punishment for painting on public property in
Chicago, Beto is sent to spend the summer with relatives in Fremont,
Utah, where he discovers that rock paintings are being looted and
decides to do something about it.
    ISBN-13: 978-1-59889-070-9 (library binding)
    ISBN-10: 1-59889-070-0 (library binding)
    ISBN-13: 978-1-59889-281-9 (paperback)
    ISBN-10: 1-59889-281-9 (paperback)
    [1. Rock paintings—Fiction. 2. Stealing—Fiction.
3. Punishment—Fiction. 4. Aunts—Fiction. 5. Uncles—Fiction.
6. Mexican Americans—Fiction. 7. Utah—Fiction.] I. Garvey,
Brann, ill. II. Title. III. Series.
PZ7.C8193Ro 2007
[Fic]—dc22
                                   2006007683

Art Director: Heather Kindseth
Graphic Designer: Kay Fraser

Photo Credits
Karon Dubke, cover (notebook and paintbrush)
Kay Fraser, cover (background images)

1 2 3 4 5 6 11 10 09 08 07 06

Printed in the United States of America

TABLE OF CONTENTS

CHAPTER 1

UTAH
TRAVELER

The silver bus shot west through the moonlit night. Beto stared out the window as the flat lands of Nebraska zipped by. He felt like his life was ruined.

His summer was, anyway.

"Sknnnx!" The man next to Beto let out a loud snore and fell toward him. He poked his shoulder, and the man fell back.

Beto relaxed a little. He opened *Zap Man Saves Chicago*.

He'd read it a million times, but still loved studying the pictures. Before long, Zap Man was a blur. Beto closed his eyes.

The bus rolled to a stop. Beto's eyes flew open. He blinked and looked out the window. The sun was up.

He looked for his bus schedule to figure out what city he was in. The snoring guy was gathering his stuff.

The bus driver yelled, "For those of you continuing on, we're stopping for two hours here in Denver. Be back on the bus by eight."

Beto watched the other travelers get off the bus. He thought about staying in Denver. It sounded a lot more exciting than going to Fremont, Utah.

Maybe he could find a job and earn enough money to go back to Chicago. Then he could hide out in the city all summer.

Of course, his mom would just call the cops to find him. He didn't need more cops in his life.

Beto stumbled off the bus, got breakfast, and cleaned up. He'd been riding since yesterday at this time, and he felt like he'd been born in his clothes.

Only nine more hours to go, he thought. He walked around until he saw the bus driver get back on the bus.

Beto took a seat in the back this time. He laid his long legs across it to stake out the whole seat.

The bus started, and Beto began to fume again about what had happened.

Why couldn't the cops see that he'd been making Chicago better, not worse? His painting on the underpass had been terrific.

His art had the same feeling Beto had felt when he first saw the paintings of Georges Rouault. Rouault's art was filled with heavy black lines and dark, rich colors.

Beto still remembered how that class trip to the Chicago Art Institute last year had changed his life.

He still couldn't believe the city had painted over his mural like it was some graffiti from a spray can.

Beto wished his art teacher could have seen it. She would have liked it.

He had painted people, all sizes and colors of people, all rushing to get somewhere.

They were larger than life, and very colorful. He had captured the movement of the city.

* * *

In a house in Fremont, Utah, the phone rang. Grace knew who it was before she picked it up.

"Are you up yet?" her mother asked.

"I am now," said Grace.

"Good. I've left clean sheets in Joy's room for Beto. Please make up his bed. And clean the bathroom. Then I left twenty dollars and a grocery list. You can walk to the store or ride your bike."

Grace hung up the phone. She felt like Cinderella. Her older sister, Joy, was gone for the summer. She had an exciting summer job in Salt Lake City, where she went to college.

Now, their mom expected Grace to do all the work around the house. And her loser cousin, Beto, who she hadn't even seen since she was three, was being dumped on her for the summer.

To top it all off, Beto was some sort of convict, or something.

Her mom called back around noon.

"I got it all done," said Grace. "Can I go swimming with Audrey?"

"Yes," her mom said, "but you have to be home at five to meet Beto at the bus station with us."

"Why do I have to go to the bus station?" Grace asked.

"You need to be there to show him that he's welcome here," her mother said.

"Well, he isn't welcome," said Grace. "I don't want him here."

"You will treat Beto kindly, or you'll spend the summer in the house," her mom said. "Beto needs to know that his family isn't judging him for getting into trouble."

"Sure we are," said Grace. "He's bad. He painted graffiti all over Chicago. You just want me to keep an eye on him, so he won't paint Fremont."

Her mom sighed. She said, "Grace Isabel Gonzales . . ."

"Okay, Mom. Fine. I'll be back by five," Grace said.

"Don't forget," her mom said.

Grace wished she could.

* * *

Aunt Helen, Grace, and Uncle Felix saw a tall, thin boy with short black hair step off the bus. He was wearing a black T-shirt, black jeans, and sneakers.

Helen and Felix pushed through the small crowd to him. Grace followed slowly.

Beto's head was spinning from being on the bus. He was hungry, tired, dirty, bored, and in no mood to talk.

"Hey Beto!" Uncle Felix pumped his hand and threw an arm across his back.

"You look just like I did at your age — tall and skinny. Look what you have to look forward to!" Uncle Felix patted his belly and slapped Beto on the back.

Beto flew forward, right into Aunt Helen's outstretched arms.

"Beto!" Aunt Helen said, a little too sweetly. "Good to see you!"

She patted Beto on the back and turned to the girl standing beside her.

The girl looked just like a young Aunt Helen. They had the same button nose, blonde ponytail, and bright green eyes.

"Remember your cousin Grace? I know you two haven't seen each other since you were in diapers," Aunt Helen said.

Beto blushed and Grace glared at her mother. The two cousins shook hands and looked past each other.

"Let's go home," Uncle Felix said. "I'm sure you'd like to unpack. We're cooking out tonight. Do you like hamburgers?"

Beto nodded. He grabbed his bag from the space under the bus and followed his uncle to the minivan.

At the house, Aunt Helen showed Beto his room. "It's probably a little too pink for you," she said, laughing, "but I think you'll be comfortable here. I emptied some drawers and made some space in the closet. Settle in, and then come for supper in half an hour."

In the kitchen, Helen said, "Grace, set the table, please."

She turned to her husband and said, "Beto certainly has grown up in the last few years. He seems like a nice, quiet boy. He doesn't look like he'll be any trouble. What do you think, Felix?"

Felix shook his head.

"I'm just glad my sister is letting us help," he said. "She has enough on her hands trying to work two jobs this summer so that Jenna can go to college in the fall. Jenna is working like a dog, too. They don't need a wild teenager on their hands."

Helen nodded. "I don't think Beto is wild," she said. "I just think he needs some guidance. It has to be hard on a boy to grow up without a dad in the house. We need to help. That means you, too, Grace."

Grace looked up from the table. "I still don't see why I have to be the baby-sitter," she said. "He's three months older than me!"

"Lower your voice," her mother said. "Beto will hear you."

"I don't care. It's not fair," said Grace.

She headed out of the kitchen just as Beto walked into the room.

"Come on, Beto," said Uncle Felix. "Let's get those hamburgers on the grill. You must be starving."

CHAPTER 2

WHAT'S THERE TO DO IN UTAH?

Beto slept for fourteen hours that night. When he finally woke up, it was noon.

He went downstairs to an empty house. In the kitchen, he made himself a sandwich and took it out to the patio. Grace was out there with her friend Audrey. They were doing cartwheels and dancing to CDs.

Beto ate his sandwich in the shade. The music was so loud that his cousin didn't hear him come out.

She twirled around and then let out a yip when she saw him. "How long have you been there?" she asked.

"Just got here," said Beto.

"You could let people know you're around," said Grace.

Beto shrugged. "I'm around."

Audrey did a cartwheel up to Beto. "We're making up new cheers for our squad. I'm Audrey. Grace's friend."

"Uh, yeah. That's great," said Beto, looking past them. "So, where's downtown?"

"Downtown?" Audrey giggled. "There's really just one street. I wouldn't call it downtown."

"What's there to do?" he asked.

"We go swimming a lot," said Grace.

"I don't swim," said Beto.

"We go on hikes," Grace added. "I practice cheerleading. Of course, there's TV. Or I could take you to the library where Mom works."

Beto didn't say anything, but he didn't have to. The expression on his face showed what he thought of this town of 5,000 people.

* * *

Downtown was two rows of buildings along Main Street. The library was a small cement building at the end of one of the rows.

Aunt Helen was the head librarian. She was also the only librarian. The other people who worked there were all volunteers.

Grace showed Beto the graphic novel section. There were five books. He had read them all. He looked through them anyway.

Grace wandered over to the checkout desk, where her mom was sorting books.

"I have nothing in common with him," Grace said.

"Does he like swimming?" Helen asked.

Grace rolled her eyes. "He doesn't swim," she said.

"Well, I guess he doesn't want to practice cheerleading." Her mom laughed.

Grace narrowed her eyes and shook her head. "Not funny," she said.

"How about a hike in the mountains?" Helen suggested.

Grace walked over to Beto. "Want to go for a hike?" she asked.

"Sure," said Beto. He got up.

"Not today," said Grace. "We can go in the morning. It will take us all day. We need to get ready."

"Okay," said Beto.

He went back to looking at the graphic novels. He was thinking that two months in Fremont, Utah, would seem like two hundred years.

Grace was thinking that two months with Beto would seem like two hundred years.

* * *

By ten o'clock the next day, the two cousins were on their way to the mountains. Aunt Helen had packed backpacks with lunch and drinks. Beto rode Joy's bike out to the foothills, where they began their hike.

Beto walked quickly. "You better slow down or you'll get tired," said Grace.

"Not me," said Beto. "I walk all over the streets of Chicago."

"And we have to watch for landmarks or we could get lost," Grace said. "We're not on a trail here."

Beto didn't seem to hear. He marched ahead, walking quickly. Grace had to run to keep up. Soon they were in the hills, and Beto was slowing down. He wasn't used to the elevation. He was starting to feel dizzy.

He didn't want to admit anything to Grace, so he stopped to examine a cactus. When he bent over, everything was spinning.

Kerplunk! His knees buckled. He fell on his knees into the cactus.

Grace tried not to laugh, but it came out anyway. She held out her hand to Beto and pulled him out of the cactus.

Beto sat down, and Grace helped him pull spines out of his jeans.

"You probably still have some stuck in you," said Grace. "It's a good thing you had jeans on. Do you want to go home?"

Beto's legs stung, but he wasn't going to act like a baby about it.

"I'm fine," he said.

"Okay," said Grace. "Go behind that rock and check to see if there are any cactus spines underneath your jeans that we missed."

Beto went behind the rock and checked his legs. He carefully pulled out a few more cactus spines. Then he saw something strange on the ground. It was a shiny black stone, about two inches long.

He showed it to Grace. "I found this sticking out of the ground. It doesn't look like any other rock around here," said Beto.

Grace took the stone and examined it. "It might have belonged to the Fremont people," she said. "They lived here, like, a thousand years ago."

"Where are they now?" Beto asked.

"Nobody knows," said Grace. "They disappeared hundreds of years ago. You need to put that stone back, or we have to give it to a ranger. It's a federal crime to take stuff from here."

"It's just a rock," said Beto as he rolled it around in his hand. He liked the way it felt. Maybe it had been used for hunting. It was exciting to think that he was holding something that was a thousand years old.

"You could go to jail for taking that stone," said Grace. "Aren't you already in enough trouble?"

Beto pushed the stone deep into his pocket. "It's just a rock," he said. He started walking again.

"Don't say I didn't warn you," Grace called after him.

CHAPTER 3

LOOTERS

Although neither one of them would have admitted it, Grace and Beto were having a good time. Grace screamed when the quick movement of a small animal startled her. Beto laughed as lizards and spiders scuttled out of their way.

Once, Beto almost tripped over a snake. The snake had just swallowed something large and couldn't move. Grace told Beto that the snake was poisonous. He was lucky the snake hadn't been able to move.

A fox ran past them. On a ledge above them, Beto thought he saw a cougar.

"If you did see one, it's a good thing you saw it before it saw you," said Grace. "Cougars sneak up on people from behind and attack them. They attack people who are walking alone."

"So you're protecting me from a cougar?" Beto laughed.

"In a way," said Grace. "I'm pretty sure we're safe. Cougars only attack people when the balance of nature is out of whack. You know, when their food supply is low. There hasn't been a report of a cougar attack for a long time. I think we're safe."

"As long as we cover each other's backs," Beto said. He smiled.

"Yeah," said Grace. "I wouldn't be out here by myself."

As they hiked, Grace told stories about people being attacked by cougars or bitten by poisonous snakes. When she ran out of stories about real animals, she began telling stories about Big Foot.

Beto listened for a while. Soon Grace's voice became a buzz in the background. Everything was so wild and open. Beto had never felt this way before. He felt like an explorer, and he imagined he was seeing things human eyes had never seen. He was walking where no person had ever walked.

In Chicago, every step Beto took was on top of the footsteps of millions of people. Beto didn't need a cougar attack to make his day. Being in the real outdoors was exciting enough for him.

They saw cliffs and valleys and rock towers. Grace kept thinking she would recognize something from another hike.

Everything she saw today seemed brand new. She knew that rangers patrolled the area, so she figured she and Beto were fine.

After a while, she noticed the shadows were getting long. She knew it would take as long to get out of the hills as it had taken to get in. And they couldn't retrace their path, because they hadn't marked it.

"Beto," said Grace, "I think we're lost. I don't know how to get out of here."

"I thought you knew this place," said Beto.

"I know some trails, but this isn't a trail. You just started walking and now we're lost."

"So now what?" Beto asked. "Try your mom's cell phone."

"It doesn't work here. We're out of range. Too many hills, I guess. Anyway, the cell phone wouldn't help. Even if I could talk to somebody, I couldn't tell them where we are."

Beto spied a tall cliff. "Let's climb that," he said. "I bet we can see everything from there. And the rangers might be able to see us."

It took almost half an hour to climb the steep cliff. When they reached the top, they were shaking from the climb. And they were out of food and water.

Nearby, Beto noticed a cave and walked toward it. Inside the cave, the walls were covered with beautiful pictures of people, animals, and symbols.

The pictures were carved into the rock with thick, strong lines. They reminded Beto of his own art. The people were big and square with broad shoulders. The pictures weren't realistic, but they weren't stick figures.

Beto's heart hammered, and he felt light-headed again. This time, his dizziness wasn't from the elevation.

He realized he was looking at art from a thousand years ago. He felt an instant connection. Someone, centuries ago, had done the same thing he did. They painted a story on walls.

"Look!" Grace said, pointing out off the cliff. About half a mile away, people were loading something into an old gray truck.

Grace waved and yelled. The people stopped moving for a moment. Then they went on loading the bed of the truck.

"Good. They'll come pick us up when they're done loading," said Grace.

Beto wasn't listening. He said, "We have to come back here with a camera. I bet no one has seen this in hundreds of years."

Grace pointed to the truck. "If we hurry, we can make it to the bottom by the time they get here to pick us up."

The climb down was harder than the climb up. Going up, they had been able to see the step ahead of them. But going down, they had to feel with their feet where the next ledge was.

By the time they reached the bottom, it was dark.

As Beto's foot hit the ground, a light flashed on them.

"What are you kids doing here?" a tall man in a ranger uniform asked.

"We're lost," said Grace.

"We're exploring," said Beto.

"Which is it?" the ranger asked.

"Both," said Grace. Beto nodded.

"Come with me," the ranger said.

"Were you looking for us because my parents reported us missing?" Grace asked.

"No. We're looking for looters," the ranger said. "Some of the rock art in this area has been damaged."

"I think we saw the looters," said Beto.

"We saw some people over there, loading something into a gray truck," said Grace. She pointed toward where the truck had been.

Beto thought about the stone in his pocket. Would the ranger think that taking a little stone was looting?

CHAPTER 4

BETO'S PLANS

On the drive back to the rangers' station, the ranger took a call on a handset. He hung up and turned to Beto and Grace. "Your parents called the station," he said. "They'll be out to pick you up soon."

The station was empty except for another ranger when they arrived.

"So tell me again what you kids were doing on a Fremont site in the dark," the ranger who'd found them said. He poured them each a glass of water.

"We were trying to find a way out," Grace explained. "We were lost."

"How far up that cliff did you get?" the ranger asked.

"We got to the top. There are cave paintings up there," said Beto.

"Did you know this is restricted land?" the ranger asked. "No one is supposed to be on this land without a permit. We're going to have to search you. When your parents get here, I'll check your backpacks and pockets."

Grace looked at her cousin. She knew the rangers would find Beto's stone. They would think she was guilty, too.

She wanted Beto to take the stone out of his pocket and hand it to the rangers.

She wanted him to explain that he didn't understand what the stone was.

She glared at her cousin, but he ignored her. He was acting like nothing was wrong.

When her parents arrived, the ranger searched the kids. And just as Grace had feared, he found the stone in Beto's pocket. "Where did you get this?" the ranger asked.

Beto shrugged. "I found it on the ground behind a big rock. I don't know where."

"This is serious business. This stone is a Fremont artifact," the ranger said. "First of all, you shouldn't have been off the trail. And secondly, taking property from these lands is a crime. I'm going to keep this here. And I have to warn you to stay out of the area you were found in. Visitors are only allowed on marked trails. There are signs posted at the park entrance that tell you not to go further. You disobeyed those signs."

"We didn't see any signs," said Grace.

The ranger ignored her. "This is a warning," he said. "If you're caught in that area again, you will be arrested for trespassing."

On the way home, Grace stared out the window. She felt horrible. Her parents hadn't been angry, but she felt like they were disappointed in her.

Beto stared out the other window. He tried to freeze the images of the cave paintings in his mind.

Aunt Helen turned in the front passenger seat and looked at Beto. "Archaeologists only recently found the Fremont artifacts here. In fact, the land you two were on is a private ranch. It's pretty exciting to know that history is being discovered in our back yard."

"The Fremont are known for their rock art," she went on. "They made a special kind of pottery, too."

"We have to leave those things alone, know what I mean, Beto?" Uncle Felix added. "There's a big question about what happened to the Fremont people. The work that the archaeologists are doing might answer that question. The reason people aren't allowed on that land is to let them do that work."

Aunt Helen nodded. "Besides, they're learning how people lived a thousand years ago. It's so fascinating! This is just about the only place in the country with ancient sites like that, that no one has studied."

In the back seat, Beto nodded. Did they think he didn't get it?

Grace stole a glance at her cousin. He had a look of determination on his face, like he couldn't wait to go back.

The next morning, Grace stayed in bed. She was exhausted from the day before.

Cheerleading camp started the next day, and Grace planned to rest up. That was a good enough excuse to keep Beto out of her hair for the day.

Hiking had been fun, until it ended with them getting into trouble. She would do all she could to keep her distance from him for the rest of the summer.

Beto had his own plans. He bought a disposable camera and a sketchbook at the drugstore. He drew what he could remember of the Fremont rock art.

Then he searched for "Fremont" on the Internet. He found pictures of rock art showing people hunting and dancing.

He also looked up information about prehistoric rock art and looters. He learned that looters had damaged many of the Fremont sites.

Beto didn't know much about his ancestors. Maybe they had once painted on rock walls.

After dinner, Uncle Felix was reading the newspaper in the living room. Beto sat down across from him. "Uncle Felix?" he asked. "Can I ask you a question?"

Uncle Felix laid down the paper and looked at Beto. "Sure, Beto. Fire away."

"Where does our family come from?"

Uncle Felix leaned back and stretched. He thought a moment before he spoke. "Well, my grandfather came up from Mexico in about 1920. Things were a little rough down there back then. Lots of people came to the United States. My grandfather became a tanner. He worked in a tannery in Chicago. Our family has lived around Chicago ever since. Except for me, of course."

"Before that, well, I don't know anything about our family before that. When we changed languages, from Spanish to English, I think we lost a lot of family stories. That history is pretty much gone."

Uncle Felix rubbed his eyes. "Your father's family came from Mexico, too, but I think they came north more recently. Is that what you wanted to know?"

Beto sighed. "Actually, I was really wondering about the Native American part of our family."

"Oh, gosh." Uncle Felix laughed. "That goes back hundreds of years. And I don't know how you'd ever find out. People didn't keep records back then."

Uncle Felix went back to his paper. Beto stood up to leave. His uncle put his paper back down. "Do you play golf, Beto?"

Beto turned. "I've never tried."

"Would you like to come with me? We can play next Saturday morning."

"Okay," said Beto.

Uncle Felix reached into his back pocket and pulled out a wad of money. He peeled off a twenty-dollar bill and handed it to Beto.

"Go to Dave's Driving Range out on Walnut Street. It's on the west edge of town. About a ten-minute walk. Tell Dave you're my nephew and ask him to show you how to hold a golf club. Get a couple of buckets of balls and practice driving them. That'll get you ready for next week. Then I can give you some pointers while we're playing."

CHAPTER 5

THE CHASE

On Saturday morning, Beto woke up before dawn. He rode Joy's bicycle to the spot where he and Grace had started their hike. This time, as he walked through the valley, he watched for landmarks. He wondered if rock art was all around him, in hidden caves and on cliff ledges.

He had two goals. First, he planned to find the cliff he and Grace had climbed and take pictures of the art. Next, he would find the people in the gray truck.

Out of the corner of his eye, Beto saw a movement on a ledge above him. He remembered Grace's warning about hiking alone. He had been so excited about his plans that he had forgotten about the cougars. He sped up.

Beto kept his eyes on the cliffs overhead. He could hear a slight noise and stopped. It continued. Cougars were quiet, so he put that fear out of his head and scanned the area.

In the distance, a man and woman were partly hidden by a huge rock. They seemed to be digging. Beto flattened himself against a tall rock and watched them.

The man stopped and took a drink from a bottle of water. He passed the bottle to the woman, who took a drink, too. They walked around and pointed to different places on the ground.

Beto watched as they went back to their work. They must be looters, he thought. He'd never make it past them without being noticed. The canyon was too narrow. He would have to climb the cliff and pass them from above.

Beto backtracked until he found a spot where he could climb. As he crept along the ledge, he figured he was about fifty feet above them. They shoveled quickly. Occasionally, one of them bent over to pick up something and throw it into a box.

Beto concentrated hard on walking quietly so he wouldn't make a noise.

A small lizard darted in front of him. He jerked back, and a rock fell.

Beto ducked down, but it was too late. The woman nudged her companion and pointed directly at him.

Beto inched backward along the ledge. He stayed low, hoping the people couldn't see him. When he got to the place where he had climbed up, he turned and looked below him. He didn't see anyone, so he started working his way down.

Just as Beto's feet hit the ground, a man jumped toward him. Beto darted back out of the canyon. He ran past large rocks and jumped over small ones.

The man was right behind him. Beto could hear him breathing. Suddenly, Beto caught a glimpse of the man's hand reaching over his shoulder. He heard the man trip and hit the ground.

Beto kept running.

He was relieved to make it to the bike, but he knew he couldn't slow down. He jumped on, and pumped as hard as he could.

It was still early morning. From a ranger lookout, the tall, thin park ranger pointed his telescope toward Beto.

He recognized the boy who had taken the rock the other day.

Before he got to town, Beto turned down a side road and found a shady spot under a tree to rest and think. His heart was beating harder than it ever had. He sank to the ground and closed his eyes.

Beto was pretty sure the man and woman were looters. They seemed to be in a hurry. Archaeologists would be more careful in their digging and take their time.

How could he know for sure?

Beto knew that if he told the rangers he'd been back on the land, he'd just get into trouble. And he couldn't prove that the other people had been there.

Then Beto remembered that the man and woman had been digging.

He needed to go back and see what the spot looked like. Maybe that could be his proof. He'd lead the rangers to that spot. But would they think he had done the digging?

Beto sat under the tree until his heart stopped pumping so hard and his skin had cooled off. Then he remembered the money his uncle had given him and he rode to Walnut Street. He paid for a bucket of golf balls and asked to speak to Dave.

Beto introduced himself to the tall, thick man and said, "My Uncle Felix told me to have you show me how to hold and swing a golf club."

"Sure, I can do that," Dave said. He led Beto to a spot and showed him.

Beto tried to copy his motions. He felt awkward. When he did manage to hit the golf ball, it only rolled a few feet.

Dave stood beside him and showed him again. Beto tried to copy him, but his heart and mind weren't helping. Dave showed him another time. Beto tried again. And again. And again.

Finally, Dave said, "Keep it up, kid. It just takes concentration."

Beto couldn't concentrate. He was thinking about the man who had chased him. Had he been hurt when he tripped?

Could Beto be charged with anything even though he hadn't actually touched the man?

Beto tried to focus on the golf ball, but his mind was too busy worrying.

CHAPTER 6

THE GAME OF GOLF

The next weekend at the golf course, Beto watched as Uncle Felix swung his club and hit the ball down the center of the fairway.

Now it was Beto's turn. They were on the third hole, and so far the score was Beto: 28, Uncle Felix: 12.

Beto put his golf ball on the tee and stood back to look at his target.

The green seemed like it was at least a mile away.

"Okay, remember," Uncle Felix coached him. "Eyes on the ball. Bend your knees just a little. Kind of sit into it a little. Got it? Okay, do a practice swing."

Beto did a practice swing and then took a step toward the tee.

"That swing looked pretty good," Uncle Felix said. "See if you can hit the ball now."

Beto swung. His club hit the ball, and it flew up into the air until he couldn't see it anymore. It went into some tall grass on the right side of the fairway.

"Good!" Uncle Felix said. "That was long. You've definitely got the distance. You just need to focus on the target."

Beto picked up Uncle Felix's old bag of clubs and slung it over his shoulder. Uncle Felix had a cart on wheels for carrying his own, newer golf clubs.

"If I play later in the day, I have to use a cart because so many people are on the course," he had told Beto. "But I love getting up early in the morning and enjoying the outdoors. It's good exercise." Then, Uncle Felix had patted his belly, as if to show that playing golf was making it smaller.

Beto walked across the fairway and hunted in the grass for his ball.

He felt like a rich kid. In Chicago, he had never even thought about playing golf. It was too expensive.

Beto found his golf ball. He couldn't hit it in the tall grass, so he placed it at the edge of the grass. That cost him an extra stroke. He took his time sizing up his shot. When he was ready, he swung.

The ball sped forward and landed on the green beyond Uncle Felix's ball.

"Great shot!" Uncle Felix called. When Beto reached the green, Felix slapped him on the back. "You're starting to look like a golfer. You just need to practice."

Beto grinned. "What does a golfer look like?" he asked.

Uncle Felix rubbed his chin. "Well, tall and thin. Of course, that's not me anymore, but it used to be. Also, you need to be a thinker. Golfers need to connect with the ball. It's kind of like playing pool. You have to think about the physics."

"I don't know physics," Said Beto.

"You probably know more about physics than you think," Uncle Felix said. "Life teaches you some of the same things you learn in school. You just don't know the names for them. Sometimes you don't know the reasons for them. It all works somehow."

He took a flag out of the cup and laid it beside the edge of the green.

Beto pulled the putter out of his golf bag. It took him five putts to sink the golf ball in the cup.

They played eighteen holes that morning. Uncle Felix gave Beto the scorecard. "Keep these cards, and you'll see your score going down over time," he advised.

Then Uncle Felix went on, "Want to play next week? This is great for me. I've never been able to get Joy or Grace interested in golf. When you're a little better, we'll play with my golf buddies."

"Sure, thanks!" said Beto.

Uncle Felix handed him another twenty-dollar bill. "Here. Go down to Dave's and hit more golf balls this week."

CHAPTER 7

HELPING OUT

When Beto got home, Aunt Helen asked him to go to the grocery store with her.

Beto slipped into the passenger's seat, and Aunt Helen started the motor. As she backed down the driveway, she began to talk.

"Beto, this is a very small town. You can't do much without someone finding out."

"What did I do?" Beto asked.

Aunt Helen looked over at him.

"I was talking to my friend Sharon today. She mentioned that she had seen you riding a bike back from the mountains a couple of days ago. Did you go back out there?"

Beto didn't move. He looked ahead.

"I can't stand lies," Aunt Helen said. "Were you back in that restricted area?"

Beto nodded. "I think I saw looters, but I'm not sure," he said.

"Did you report it?" Aunt Helen asked.

Beto shook his head.

"Why not?" Aunt Helen asked.

Beto didn't know what to say.

When Aunt Helen was done shopping, they loaded the groceries into the car and drove home without speaking.

As they pulled into the driveway, Aunt Helen turned to Beto.

"You need to call the rangers and tell them what you saw, and then you need to stay off that land. To keep yourself out of trouble, you can help me around the house while Grace finishes cheerleading camp."

"Yes, ma'am," said Beto.

* * *

For the next week, he dusted, vacuumed, mopped floors, cleaned bathrooms, and helped Aunt Helen prepare meals.

In his spare time, he watched TV, practiced his golf swing, and read more about the Fremont rock artists on the Internet. He drew more sketches in his sketchbook, too.

Beto thought about the looters, too. He called the ranger station, but only got an answering machine. He left a message describing the looters and saying where they were, but he didn't leave his name.

Beto felt like Aunt Helen was taking advantage of him. He wished he could call his mom and tell her about it. But he knew his mom would just tell him to buck up.

He liked Uncle Felix. He felt sorry for his uncle. He was stuck with Aunt Helen forever.

Grace left the house each morning before Beto got up. In the evenings, she talked on the phone with her friends or went to someone's house.

Beto figured Aunt Helen now thought he was a bad influence. She didn't want her precious daughter around him.

* * *

"After you finish mowing the yard tomorrow, why don't you visit me at the library?" Aunt Helen said on Thursday night. "I have something to show you."

"Okay," said Beto.

Beto was too tired to ask what it was. He figured she'd probably gotten a new graphic novel in.

Or she wanted him to shelve books because she was running out of work for him to do at home.

The next day, Aunt Helen showed Beto a small section in the library devoted to the Fremont people and their culture.

"This section contains almost everything that's been printed about the Fremont," Aunt Helen explained.

"There isn't much, but because this was their home too, we try to keep up. Sometimes archaeologists stop here to study. It helps, since most people aren't actually allowed to see much of the park."

She paused, and then added, "I thought you might want to see it."

"I do," said Beto. "What do you mean that people aren't allowed to see much of the park? Can they see some of it?"

"I think there are ways for people to see some of the rock art. But you might as well forget it. Those park rangers don't want to see you again. These books are probably as close as you can get."

The books were interesting, but some were very difficult. Still, Beto read each book, whether he understood it or not. He read some parts over many times, trying to understand what they said. He hoped the information was sinking into his brain.

He had seen Aunt Helen looking at him. He was sure that if he weren't here reading about the Fremont, she'd have him painting the house or digging a hole for a swimming pool in the back yard.

Except for playing golf Saturday morning, Beto spent the weekend at the library, studying and sketching.

By Monday, Aunt Helen had changed her mind about Beto. As she watched him study the Fremont books, she got an idea. She decided to convince the rangers to let him go to the site again. She would go with him.

Sitting at the wooden library table, Beto decided to take matters into his own hands. He would go to the site again.

And he'd go alone.

CHAPTER 8

GONE FISHING

Once cheerleading camp was over, the rest of the long summer stretched out in front of Grace. With Beto around, she had fewer chores to do. But after a while, she started feeling sorry for him. He must be pretty bored, she thought, having to hang out with her dad and help out her mom all the time.

Uncle Felix thought Beto was bored, too. He thought of another hobby he wanted to teach his nephew. "Hey, Beto, we'll go fishing on Sunday, okay?"

Beto nodded, even though he thought fishing sounded pretty pointless. Couldn't they buy fish at the grocery store? He wrote his mom a letter and told her. He knew it would make her happy that he was bonding with Uncle Felix.

Grace and Felix were wrong about Beto being bored. He had been very busy. He'd made a map of the state land in his sketchbook. He used maps from the library to help. He figured a way to get back in to the rock art cave without being seen. The trick would be finding a time when no one at home would miss him.

So on Sunday, Beto and Uncle Felix went fishing. Beto was amazed at how hard it was. Hours later, they went home without any fish.

"That was kind of like playing golf," Beto said. "It's another dream for me."

Uncle Felix laughed. "Just like golf, fishing takes patience. If you want to get into some flyfishing, you can practice casting. I got you a license, so you can fish anytime you want to. On the way home I'll show you a stream that's closer. You can bike there."

Beto nodded. He wanted to fish some more. It had been kind of fun to sit out on the water, relaxing. He would practice. And unless he got caught, if he said he was going fishing, people wouldn't bother him. He didn't plan on getting caught.

A few days later, when Aunt Helen and Uncle Felix had just left for work, and while Grace was still asleep, Beto made his move.

He tied the fishing pole to the bike's frame. Then he packed a lunch and a disposable camera. He rode his bike toward the stream Uncle Felix had pointed out. It was right on the edge of the state land.

Beto had memorized the map he had drawn. He passed the stream and kept riding toward the hills. It was a beautiful day. Beto realized that he was starting to like Utah. It wasn't as exciting as Chicago, but it was cool.

Beto rode into the valley and hid the bike behind some large rocks. He figured out which way was north by looking at the position of the sun. Then he started walking into the restricted land, noting landmarks along the way. He figured that he could be out there all day. He was in no hurry, and no one was around. So he was surprised to see tire tracks in the dirt.

As Beto entered a valley, he spotted the old gray truck. He took a picture of it. He moved in close and walked around the back of the truck. The license plate was spattered with mud, so he wiped it off and snapped another picture.

Beto wondered what to do next. If he kept going, there was a good chance that he'd run into whoever the truck belonged to. He decided to go west, away from the main trail. He walked for about ten minutes.

But on a hunch, he turned around and went back toward the truck.

As Beto neared the truck, he heard a scraping noise. He crouched behind a rock. The scraping noise grew louder.

A man was pushing a wheelbarrow straight toward Beto. A woman was walking beside him, steadying the contents of the wheelbarrow.

Looking at the man's face, Beto was pretty sure that it was the same guy who had chased him.

Then Beto looked more closely at the wheelbarrow. It contained a huge rock.

And as the looters came closer, Beto could see that the rock was covered with Fremont rock art!

Every nerve in Beto's body was on fire. How could someone destroy this treasure?

Beto grabbed his camera and jumped up. He snapped a photo of the pair with the wheelbarrow and their loot. Then he turned and ran through the valley toward Joy's bike. He didn't wait around to see the pair cover their treasure with a tarp, jump into the truck, and take off after him.

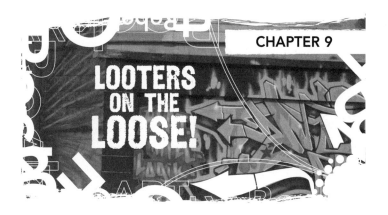

CHAPTER 9

LOOTERS ON THE LOOSE!

Beto scrambled up a hill to hide among some rocks and wait for the truck to pass. In less than five minutes, he saw the truck coming toward him.

The woman was driving, and the man was sitting in the back of the truck scouring the hills for signs of a running boy.

Beto ducked. His blood was racing. He didn't dare move. The truck moved through the canyon slowly.

Beto heard a door creak open and then slam shut. There was complete silence for about fifteen minutes.

Beto sat like a statue, listening for sounds of movement. Then he heard the crunch of tires on the earth. He waited until he couldn't hear the truck's motor anymore.

When Beto raised his head above the rocks to look, the man was standing in the opening to the canyon looking through binoculars. He seemed to be looking directly at Beto. Beto ducked back down and hoped that the man hadn't seen him.

He didn't hear any footsteps getting nearer. Just to be safe, he sat quietly for two long hours before he dared to look again.

The man was gone. Beto made his way to the canyon opening. The truck was gone. His bike was gone, too.

It was several miles into town. Those miles were wide open, and it was still daylight. The truck could be waiting for him. Beto decided that it would be safer to try to find the rangers' station.

On his way, he hiked past the spot where he'd seen the two people. There, he could see the destruction that the looters had caused.

On a ledge above him, there was a picture of ancient hunters. He could also see a huge hole where the looters had chipped and pried part of the pictures from the wall. Beto hurried past it. The looters had to be stopped before they did any more damage.

The sound of a motor broke Beto's thoughts. Was it a helicopter? He hoped that the rangers were already after the looters.

Beto ducked behind a rock just in time to see the gray truck returning.

The truck bed was empty. The man and woman got out and headed toward the chipped wall.

Beto wanted to stand up and shout at them. He wanted to stop them from causing more destruction, but he knew it wasn't safe.

He needed to get help.

Now that the looters were back inside the canyon, Beto could get out and get help. Slowly, Beto crept around the couple as they worked. When Beto reached the edge of the canyon again, he ran to the road.

Beto decided that it would be quicker to go into town than to find the rangers' station. He spent the next two hours running and walking, as fast as he could, back into town. Whenever he heard a motor sound behind him, he checked to make sure it wasn't the gray truck.

CHAPTER 10

When Beto reached his aunt and uncle's house, he burst through the door. Grace was sitting in the living room watching TV and painting her toenails. She looked at Beto. He was dripping in sweat, and he had a terrible expression on his face.

"What's wrong?" Grace asked.

"Where are your parents?" Beto panted.

"Out," she said. "They went to a dinner party in Saw Mill."

"What's that?" Beto asked.

"A dinner party is . . ."

"No! Saw Mill!"

"It's the next town over," said Grace. "There's some kind of award ceremony Dad had to go to."

Beto paced back and forth, tapping the front of his head. "Rangers!" He picked up the phone and looked at Grace. "What's the number?"

"Um, I guess the phonebook . . ."

"Help me!" he shouted. "This is an emergency!" He told Grace what had happened out on the state land.

"I have pictures!" he finished. "Proof!"

"You'd better protect them with your life," said Grace. "If there are no pictures, nobody's going to believe you."

No one answered the phone when Beto called the rangers' station.

"They're probably closed for the night," said Grace.

"Don't they stay there all the time?"

Grace shrugged. "I don't know. This has never come up before."

"We need to go back out there," said Beto.

"We can't!" said Grace. "First of all, we don't have a car. Second, it's against the law. Those people could hurt us. Do you think they were just going to tell you to be quiet? They were probably going to run you down and leave you for dead."

"Call the sheriff!" said Beto.

They called the sheriff, but he didn't seem to believe them. All he said was, "We'll see what we can do."

"Could we try to call your parents?" Beto asked his cousin.

Grace shook her head. "I tried earlier when I wanted to ask if I could go to Audrey's. That's why I'm here alone. They're out of cell phone range. I guess we could call the police there and have them locate them, but I don't know if the police would believe us. Saw Mill's a real small town, too. They might not even have a police department."

Grace looked outside. "It's dark out now," she said. "There's no moon. Those people are probably done for the night."

Beto shook his head. "They know I got away and that I'll turn them in, with pictures. They probably have powerful flashlights. And if not, they have the truck's headlights. The rangers could find them tonight by the light they're making. Tomorrow, they'll probably be out of the country."

Grace picked up the phone.

"Who are you calling?" Beto asked.

"Audrey," said Grace.

Beto exploded. "How could you call your friend at a time like this?"

"Aud? Hi. Is your dad around?" Grace asked. "Good. We have an emergency and we need a ride. Could he drive over here?"

Grace hung up the phone. "Audrey's dad is a sheriff's deputy. He can at least get us out to the ranger station," she said.

* * *

Forty minutes later, Audrey's dad, Beto, Audrey, and Grace arrived at the locked gates to the state land.

"I can't go further," Audrey's dad said. "Let's just save this for the morning."

"I wonder if a cell phone works in this spot," said Grace. She took out her cell phone to call the rangers' station again, but couldn't get a signal.

Beto jumped out of the car. "I'm walking. I can get through that fence. I know where the rangers' station is from here."

"It's a ways off," Audrey's dad said. "And there are rattlesnakes and cougars. All kinds of night hunters are out there right now. Plus, it's illegal. I think you should just wait until the morning."

Beto kept going. Grace followed him.

Audrey looked at her dad. He knew he didn't have a choice. He couldn't leave two teenagers out in the middle of nowhere. He shut off the car and grabbed a flashlight from under the seat. He and Audrey hurried after Grace and Beto.

Two rangers that Beto and Grace hadn't seen before were working at the station that night. Beto was relieved that it wasn't the one who had hauled him in before. He hoped these rangers would believe him. Beto had brought his sketchbook along to show the rangers the map he had drawn. He had also brought the camera.

After Beto told his story, one the rangers said, "That's protected territory. What were you doing there?"

"I wanted to find the looters," said Beto. "And also, I wanted to take pictures of the rock art. I wasn't going to touch anything."

The other ranger was working at a computer. She looked at the screen. "You're on our list," she said. "You have been warned to keep off this land because you are considered a threat to it. Says here that you tried to steal an artifact."

"I didn't know about the Fremont," said Beto. "I didn't know that it was a crime to take something. I would never, ever do that again," he said.

"There's a note that you might have been on the state land at other times," the ranger said. "Another ranger saw someone who fit your description leaving the area."

"I didn't mean any harm," said Beto. "That's the only other time I've been here."

"Well," the ranger said, "I'm going to have to cite you for trespassing again today. You've admitted as much."

"You have to believe me," Beto said. "You have to stop those people from doing more damage. They were chipping off huge chunks of rock art. They're probably working right now. They'll be gone by tomorrow."

He handed over the disposable camera. "There are three pictures on this camera. One is of the gray truck they are driving. One is the license plate of the truck. The third picture is of the people holding the goods. They had rock art in a wheelbarrow, and I got their picture. I got their faces, looking right into the camera. Here's my sketchbook. This map shows exactly where they are."

The rangers took the camera and Beto's sketchbook. Then the group walked back to Audrey's dad's car.

Uncle Felix and Aunt Helen arrived home just as Audrey's dad dropped off Beto and Grace. They listened to Beto's story.

Aunt Helen sighed. "Beto," she said, "I'm sorry, but you're to stay in this house. Until further notice."

CHAPTER 11

KNOWING
THE
LIMITS

Beto spent the next few days wandering around the house. He didn't know if the looters had been caught. He didn't know what had happened to the photos he had taken. As far as he knew, the camera could still be sitting on the ranger's desk. The looters could still be chipping precious art off the cliffs.

Beto tried to call the rangers' station, but he only got a recording. He left several messages, but no one called him back.

Uncle Felix was too busy to go fishing or golfing, or even to talk. He barely spoke to Beto. Beto knew that he had let his uncle down by trespassing on the state land. He wished he could explain that he thought he was doing a good thing. All he wanted to do was save the art.

It was just like what happened in Chicago. He thought he was putting something good into the world. He worked so hard to make the mural. It would have been quicker with spray paint, but he used a brush. He wanted to do it right, to be an urban artist. But everyone told him he was wrong.

When he and his mom had met with the Chicago police, it hurt Beto that she didn't understand what he had tried to do. Now Uncle Felix was siding with the rangers. Beto didn't understand why the truth was so hard for people to see.

At least Grace seemed sympathetic. She played cards with him, and they watched TV.

Aunt Helen asked Beto to do a few chores around the house. At least she wasn't treating him differently than she had before.

One night at dinner, Uncle Felix said he had news.

"Good news or bad news?" asked Grace.

"Both," Uncle Felix said. "Which do you want first?"

"Let's hear the good news first," Aunt Helen said.

"Okay," Uncle Felix said. He turned toward Beto and put his hands together. "Well, Beto, you'll be happy to know that they caught the looters. They captured them on the freeway, thanks to your photos."

Beto ducked his head and grinned.

He clenched his fists and said, "Yes!" Aunt Helen got up from her chair and walked over to give Beto a big hug.

"Are they in prison?" asked Beto.

"They have to go to trial first," Uncle Felix said. "I think they're in jail, though. There's solid proof with those pictures. You will probably need to testify."

"I'm only supposed to be here for a few more weeks," said Beto. "Will the trial happen before I go?"

"Well, you might need to stay here a while longer. Or maybe you'll come back to testify."

"What about all the Fremont stuff they stole?" Beto asked.

"They found a lot of artifacts in the truck," Uncle Felix said. "The looters weren't from this area. They were taking it home to sell it, I guess. We'll learn more at the trial."

"You said there was bad news too. What's the bad news?" Grace asked.

"Oh yes, now the bad news," Uncle Felix said. "Beto, you have to go to trial, too."

Beto gulped. "Why?"

"You know why, Beto," Uncle Felix said. "You trespassed after you were given a warning. I partly blame myself for not explaining to you how serious that warning was. You need to obey things like that."

Aunt Helen looked at Beto. "Beto, this is your fault. You made it happen. I should have made you be responsible for your own actions that second time you trespassed. I wanted everything to be okay, but I was sticking my head in the sand."

"Anyway," Uncle Felix continued, "I've talked to a lawyer today. A week from next Thursday, you will appear in juvenile court."

Beto swallowed. He seemed to be headed for a life of trouble, no matter where he went or what he did.

Beto looked at Grace. "Why isn't Grace in trouble too?" he asked.

"I didn't steal anything," said Grace. "And I didn't trespass again when I learned it was wrong. Believe me, Beto, I know the limits."

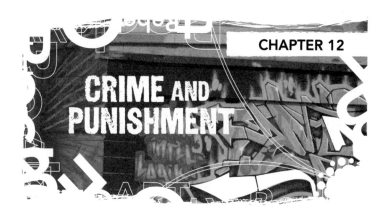

CHAPTER 12

CRIME AND PUNISHMENT

Beto sat in the courtroom. Uncle Felix was on one side of him, and Beto's lawyer sat on the other.

They listened to the ranger's testimony about Beto trespassing on restricted land.

The ranger said, "Although Beto was trespassing, he also provided important information that helped us catch some looters of Fremont artifacts."

Beto was called to the witness stand.

The lawyer asked him to explain why he had trespassed after being told to stay off the state land.

"It's hard to explain," said Beto. "I guess I had something in common with the looters. We were thinking the same thing."

Beto paused and looked over at the judge. "I think of myself as an artist, and I feel a strong tie to the Fremont art," he said. "I tried to stay away, but I thought about it all the time. And I thought about what looters could do to it. I know what it's like to lose your art. So I felt that I had to protect the art. It's simple. We were all drawn to the rock art, but for different purposes," he added.

Uncle Felix and the lawyer looked relieved.

"I wanted to keep looters away, but I also wanted to see the rock art again. I wanted to take my own pictures. But I wouldn't have touched anything," said Beto.

The prosecuting lawyer handed Beto his sketchbook. "Is this yours?" the lawyer asked.

"Yes, it is my sketchbook," said Beto.

"And this map shows how you planned to get to the rock art?" the lawyer asked.

"Yes," said Beto.

The lawyer handed the sketchbook to the judge. The judge looked through it, and then laid it down. After a few more questions, the judge called a recess.

Uncle Felix and the lawyer took Beto down the hall to the cafeteria for lunch. Beto was too nervous to eat anything.

"They didn't ask about what happened in Chicago," said Beto. "I thought they'd bring that up."

"Fortunately for you, you're a kid. That case can't be used as evidence in this trial," the lawyer said.

Beto thought about his court appearance in Chicago. His mom had to pay for the destruction the city said he had caused. Then the city had painted over his artwork.

An hour later, the judge addressed the courtroom. "We have an interesting case here. This young man tried to take a precious artifact from historic lands. He says that he didn't know that it was an artifact. He didn't realize its importance. That could be true. The young man is not from around here. We would expect young people who grew up in this area to appreciate what we have in our back yard. But we can't expect outsiders to understand until they have been taught."

She went on, "This young man here disobeyed a law at least once that we know of. He trespassed on state land after he was ordered off."

She looked at the ranger.

"And he thought he could take the law into his own hands, hunting down looters that park rangers should have found."

"Why?" she continued. "Why did Beto think that he had the right to do something that no one else is allowed to do?" The judge looked directly at Beto. "That is the heart of the problem. Why can Beto do things that no one else is allowed to do? The answer, clearly and simply, is that he can't. And for his trespassing, he must be punished."

Beto's heart stopped. The judge paused and took a sip of water, then continued.

"However, while trespassing, Beto came upon criminals in the act of a federal crime. He showed bravery and wisdom in his efforts to help catch those criminals. For his bravery and good citizenship, Beto should be rewarded. But it's not this court's place to reward him, only to punish him."

The judge folded her hands in front of her and leaned toward Beto.

"Beto, as punishment for your crime, I order that you do forty hours of community service in the town of Fremont. You said that you are an artist, and I saw your drawings in your sketchbook. They are very good, and I think your art can help the community. So, for your community service, you will paint a mural on the side of the Fremont Public Library. The mural will show how important it is to preserve the culture of the Fremont people. You will present sketch ideas for approval to a board. The board will include the mayor, the head librarian, and others of their choosing. The committee will look over your work."

Beto let out a big breath of air.

The judge stood up. Court was over.

Beto couldn't stop smiling.

Uncle Felix turned to him. "Just think, Beto, if you hadn't photographed those looters, this might all be happening in a different way."

"I know," said Beto.

Uncle Felix took an envelope out of his jacket pocket. "I've got more news. Your sentence was supposed to be the bad news, and this was the good news. But the bad news wasn't so bad after all. See what you think of the good news."

Beto took the envelope and opened it. Inside was a check for $1,000.

"It's the reward for the capture of those looters," Uncle Felix explained. "You've earned it, and I hope you will use it for something good."

Beto thought about it.

There were so many things a thousand dollars could buy. But he knew what he'd do with the money.

"I'll pay back my mom," said Beto. "For the stuff in Chicago."

He stepped out of the court building and into the afternoon sun. Beto held his sketchbook tightly to his chest.

He thought about his mother, and how happy she would be to hear how it had all turned out. He thought of the pride he felt when the judge said the looters had been caught because of what he had done.

But mostly, he thought about how excited he was to paint the mural.

Beto turned to his uncle. "I can't wait to get to work!" he said.

MORE ABOUT THE FREMONT PEOPLE

It is believed that people first came to the Utah region about 12,000 years ago. Today, those people are called the Fremont people because they lived along the Fremont River. The Fremont people began their stay in Utah as hunter-gatherers.

The Fremont people raised corn, beans, and squash along the river bottom. They lived high up in the cliffs. They hauled their grain up to the cliffs for safe storage.

The Fremont people seemed to be protecting themselves and their food. No one knows what they were afraid of.

The Fremont hunted rabbits, deer, mice, and bighorn sheep. They hunted with traps and bows and arrows.

They used every part of the animals they killed. They ate the meat and used the fur for clothing and shoes.

They also fished, using nets and fishhooks.

The Fremont people had certain ways of making objects that set them apart from other people of their time.

- They made baskets from willow, milkweed, yucca, and other fibers. The type of weaving is called "one-rod-and-bundle." No other culture used this type of basket.

- They wore a type of shoe made from the feet of deer or mountain sheep. Other cultures of that period wore sandals.

- They made a kind of thin, gray pottery. It was unlike other pottery of the time.

- They had a very decorative style of rock art. It showed people with blunt haircuts wearing many necklaces.

- They built several different types of houses, all different from the types built by the people who lived south of them.

- They sewed and wore animal skins, which the people from the south did not do.

- They raised a different type of corn than the people south of them.

The Fremont culture ended around 1250 A.D. No one knows why their culture disappeared.

It is thought that the Fremont people might have either joined or, more likely, been pushed out of the area by the Ute, Paiute, and Shoshone people.

The state of Utah has hundreds of sites where the Fremont people lived. Many sites have not yet been explored.

New rock art is still being found. All sites are protected from looters by strict laws.

⁂ ABOUT THE AUTHOR ⁂

M. J. Cosson grew up thinking that she would
become an artist. She won scholarships in
school to attend classes at the local art museum,
and her bachelor's degree is in art. She began
working as a graphic artist, then realized that
she was a better writer than artist. She lives in
Iowa with her dogs, Clancy and Clementine,
and her cat, Carrie Chapman Catt.

⁂ ABOUT THE ILLUSTRATOR ⁂

Brann Garvey grew up in the great state of Iowa.
He graduated from the Minneapolis College
of Art & Design with a degree in illustration.
Brann is usually found with one or more of the
following: a pencil in his hand, a comic book, a
remote for watching DVDs, or his pet kitty, Iggy.
When the weather is nice, Brann likes to play
disc golf, and he proudly points out that Iowa is
one of the world's centers for the sport. Iggy does
not play.

⁘ GLOSSARY ⤞

ancient (AYN-shunt)—very old, or belonging to a long time ago

cave art (KAYV ART)—paintings or sculpture on cave walls, usually created by ancient peoples

elevation (el-uh-VAY-shuhn)—a high place or hill. When a person is at a high elevation, they might suffer because the air doesn't have the right amount of oxygen.

fairway (FAIR-way)—in the game of golf, the grass between the tee and the green

foothills (FUT-hilz)—the low hills at the base of a mountain or mountain range

graffiti (gruh-FEE-tee)—pictures or words painted or drawn in public, usually illegally

looters (LOOT-urz)—people who steal

park ranger (PARK RAYN-jur)—person in charge of watching over a park or protected land

⋅⋆ DISCUSSION QUESTIONS ⋅⋆

1. Beto felt very strongly about protecting the ancient rock art, even if it meant he broke the law by walking on protected land. Do you think what Beto did was wrong? Why or why not?

2. Sometimes, it seemed as though the rangers were not listening to Beto's story. Have you ever felt as though someone wasn't listening to you? What did you do?

3. At the beginning of the book, Beto's cousin, Grace, doesn't seem to like him very much. What changes her mind about him? Do you think Beto and Grace will still be friends when Beto moves back to Chicago?

⚡ WRITING PROMPTS ⚡

1. Imagine the state lands that Beto trespassed on. Draw your version of the map Beto drew in his sketchbook, using this book to help you. Remember to include special landmarks!

2. Write (and illustrate!) your own graphic novel, like the books Beto likes.

3. The judge asks Beto to paint a mural on the Fremont library. What do you think it looks like? Draw your own version, and then write about what you drew.

⚡INTERNET SITES ⚡

Do you want to know more about subjects
related to this book? Or are you interested in
learning about other topics? Then check out
FactHound, a fun, easy way to find Internet sites.

Our investigative staff has already sniffed out
great sites for you!

Here's how to use FactHound:

1. Visit *www.facthound.com*

2. Select your grade level.

3. To learn more about subjects related
   to this book, type in the book's ISBN number:
   1598890700.

4. Click the **Fetch It** button.

FactHound will fetch the best Internet sites
for you!